T0243113

I Missed My Hugs

Corrie Harris and Debra Harris

Copyright © 2021 Corrie Harris and Debra Harris.

All rights reserved. No part of this book may be used or reproduced by any means, graphic, electronic, or mechanical, including photocopying, recording, taping or by any information storage retrieval system without the written permission of the author except in the case of brief quotations embodied in critical articles and reviews.

This is a work of fiction. All of the characters, names, incidents, organizations, and dialogue in this novel are either the products of the author's imagination or are used fictitiously.

Archway Publishing books may be ordered through booksellers or by contacting:

Archway Publishing
1663 Liberty Drive
Bloomington, IN 47403
www.archwaypublishing.com
844-669-3957

Because of the dynamic nature of the Internet, any web addresses or links contained in this book may have changed since publication and may no longer be valid. The views expressed in this work are solely those of the author and do not necessarily reflect the views of the publisher, and the publisher hereby disclaims any responsibility for them.

Any people depicted in stock imagery provided by Getty Images are models, and such images are being used for illustrative purposes only.
Certain stock imagery © Getty Images.

Interior Image Credit: Debra Harris

ISBN: 978-1-6657-0558-5 (sc)
ISBN: 978-1-6657-0559-2 (hc)
ISBN: 978-1-6657-0557-8 (e)

Print information available on the last page.

Archway Publishing rev. date: 6/4/2021

Everything looks so good outside the sun is shining and I can only enjoy the day through the window.

The Doctor on television said, "we have to stay in and distance ourselves plus wear a mask. Because there is a disease out there and people past it on to others. "They are working hard to get this sickness under control, and we must follow the rules to stay safe. We must protect ourselves and our loved ones.

I get it!

But I missed my hugs.

We cannot hug because of the p-a-n-d-e-m-i-c that big sickness that has covered the world, but I missed my hugs.

I Cannot hug my friends and I cannot hug my teacher.

I Cannot go to family gathering, boy that is where you get lots of hugs!

I Cannot hug the bus driver
and my friend across the street.

I am tired of watching my big brother from the window. Although, he leaves some great surprises on the porch. I miss his big hugs even though he carries me around by my feet. That nothing but love.

I must figure out how to get my hug back.

I got it but, I will need some help from the whole family. Audie got out his craft materials, crayons, pencils, and he drew several pictures of what his project would look like. One came out good. Now it needs a name, I will call it send -a - hug.

I will need help from the whole family. I asked mother father and sister to help.

Audie showed them a drawing of his idea. His sister asked.

What is it a doll?

He replied, "No".

Then, "what is it?"

He replied, "Send- a- hug."

I want to send a hug to all my friends. I missed my hugs.

Name of my project is

Send a hug

☐ velcrow (2) pieces

velcrow → [felt hand drawing]

Felt hand (2)

[head/mask drawing]
Line is for your name
← openings
← pocket to send a message
  mask
← Cardboard for face

mask

[cloth strip drawing]
↑ Cloth strip for arms they fold up.
  (2)

Thread to sew on arms
or
fabric glue

Send -a – Hug layout

Suggestions for Send – a- Hugs.

Dad look at my idea. He said, "not bad."

Things needed by Audie.

Cardboard 8 x 10 sheets

Felt assorted colors for the hands.

Scissors & fabric glue.

Fabric strips assorted colors or one color or (colored socks)

A roll of Velcro one-inch-wide cut into 1x1 squares is put on the hands.

Crayon or Markers

Pack of white paper for mask

A drawing table 12 x 18 the sheets are folded to make the envelopes be creative in your designs.

(A variety of Shapes)

The mask is glued to the face at the top is an opening so you can insert a note or photo inside.

Dad said, "I would like to send a hug to my grandparents a hug with my photo, great idea!"

Everyone has some paper, scissors, fabric glue, felt, cardboard, and white drawing paper.

His Sister said, "not a bad idea."

I will get some colorful fabric for my hugs.

Mother said, "this is a great family project." Sending Hugs.

Everyone working and assembling their send – a – hug.
We pack them in envelops and dad dropped them off.
Windy across the street. We put it on her porch. Zak,
and Winston we put theirs in the mailbox.

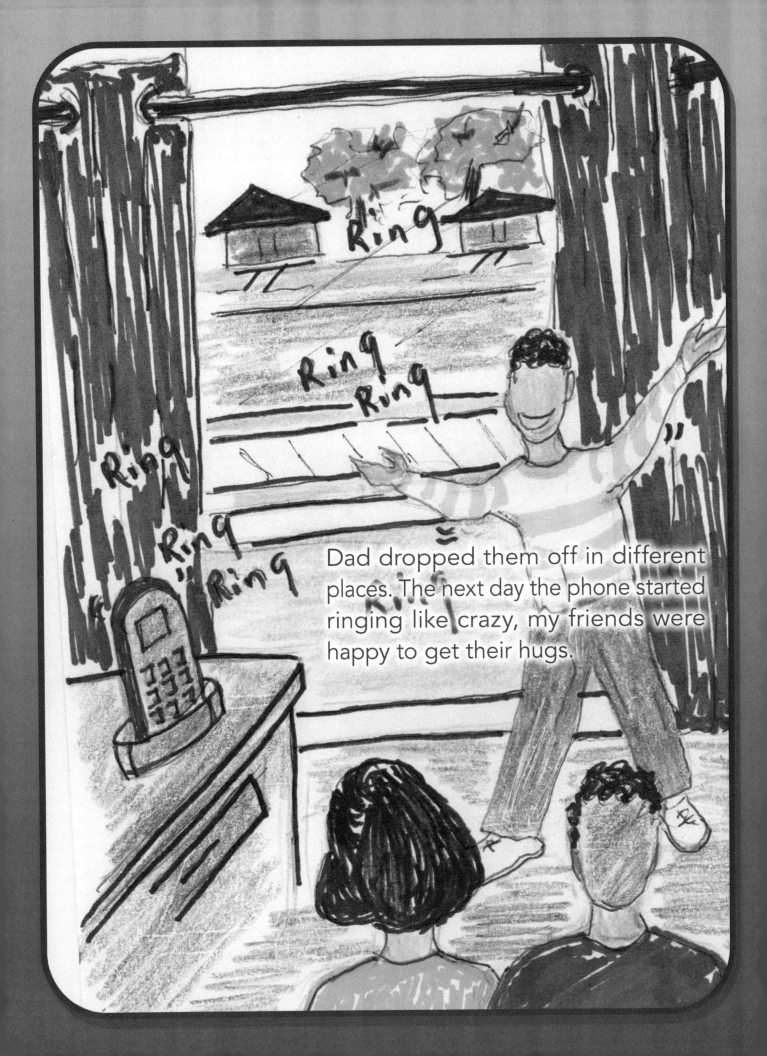

Dad dropped them off in different places. The next day the phone started ringing like crazy, my friends were happy to get their hugs.

The next day I started to receive hugs in my mailbox. I got my hugs back.

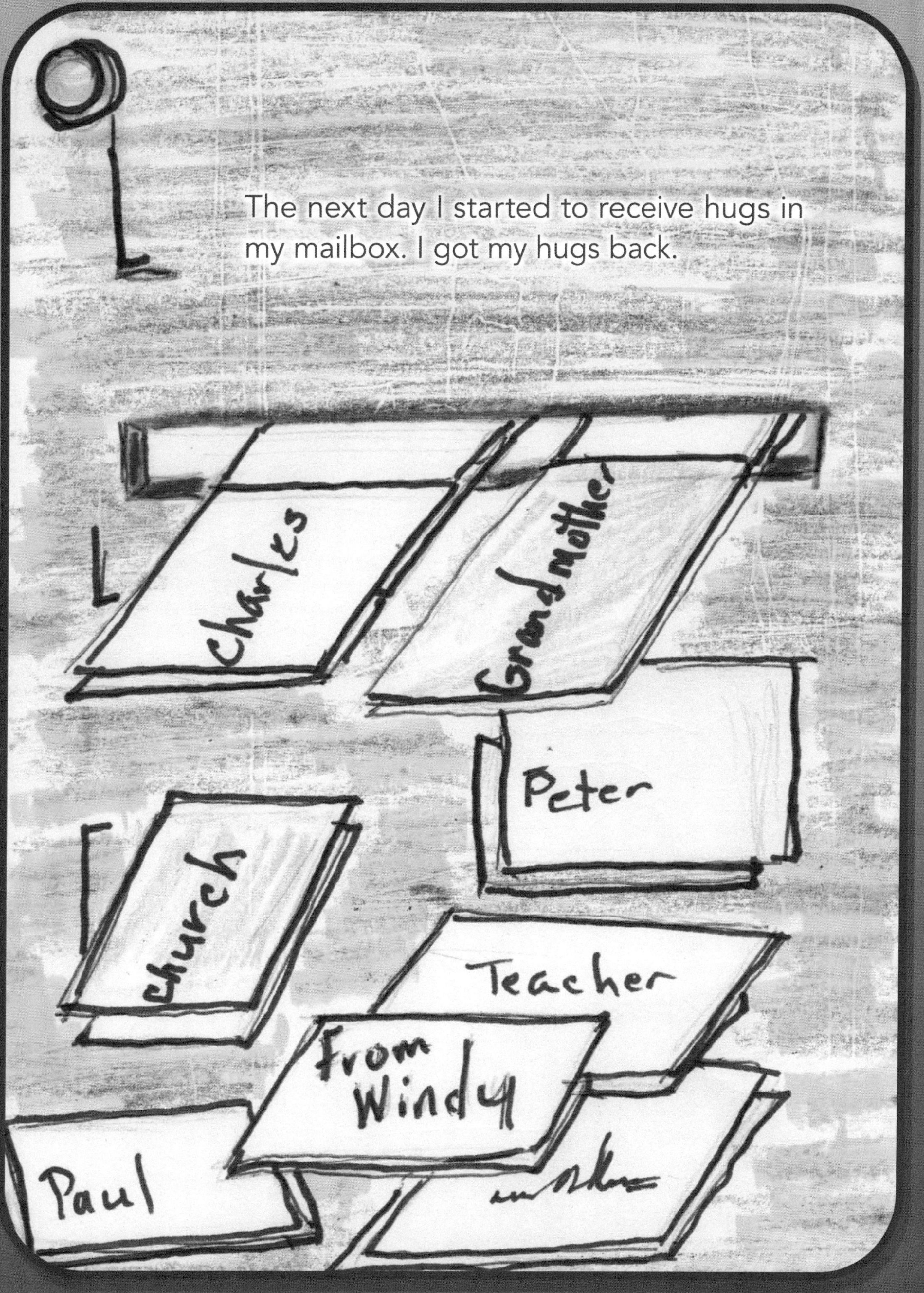

Charles

Grandmother

Peter

church

Teacher

From Windy

Paul

I looked out the window there was Windy with her hug on, and Zak even Winston in his front yard.

I put on all my hugs and stood on the porch.
Everyone was so happy. The mail man had
his hugs on too.

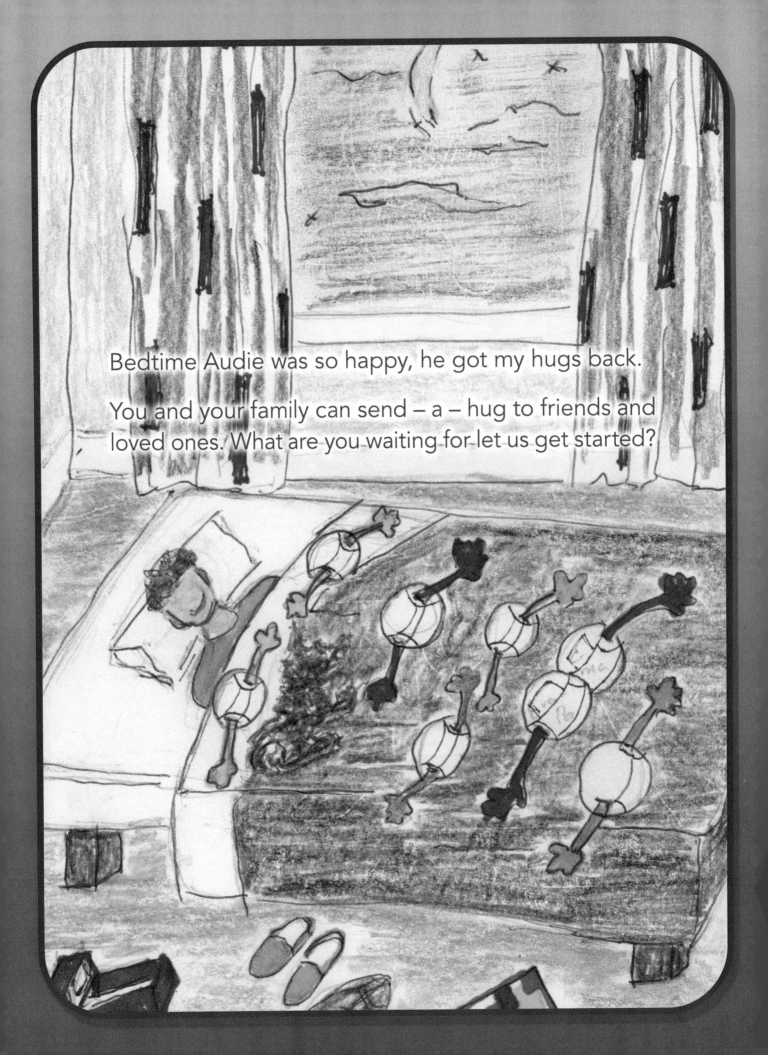

Bedtime Audie was so happy, he got my hugs back.

You and your family can send – a – hug to friends and loved ones. What are you waiting for let us get started?